For my big brothers and sisters

**BEACH LANE BOOKS**
An imprint of Simon & Schuster Children's Publishing Division
1230 Avenue of the Americas, New York, New York 10020
© 2022 by Mark Teague
Book design by Sonia Chaghatzbanian © 2022 by Simon & Schuster, Inc.
All rights reserved, including the right of reproduction in whole or in part in any form.
BEACH LANE BOOKS and colophon are trademarks of Simon & Schuster, Inc.
For information about special discounts for bulk purchases, please contact Simon & Schuster Special Sales
at 1-866-506-1949 or business@simonandschuster.com.
The Simon & Schuster Speakers Bureau can bring authors to your live event.
For more information or to book an event, contact the Simon & Schuster Speakers Bureau at 1-866-248-3049
or visit our website at www.simonspeakers.com.
The text for this book was set in NewsGothicBT.
The illustrations for this book were rendered in acrylics.
Manufactured in China
0422 SCP
First Edition
10 9 8 7 6 5 4 3 2 1
CIP data for this book is available from the Library of Congress.
ISBN 9781665912303
ISBN 9781665912310 (ebook)

# KING KONG'S COUSIN

### WRITTEN AND ILLUSTRATED BY
## MARK TEAGUE

**Beach Lane Books** • New York   London   Toronto   Sydney   New Delhi

**KONG** was the most famous gorilla in the city.

His cousin, Junior, was not famous at all.

Kong was as big as an apartment building.

Junior lived in an apartment building with
his mother and his cat, Bernice.

Kong was as strong as four elephants.

Junior was as strong as Bernice.

"Soon I will be big and strong too!" said Junior.

He did his exercises

and ate his bamboo

and marked his height on the wall.

Kong wrestled dinosaurs.

Kong climbed to the tops of skyscrapers.

Junior climbed onto his piano bench.

When Junior took a bath, it was just a bath.

When Kong took a bath, it was an extravaganza!

Kong did heroic things.

Junior did chores.

He fed his goldfish, Larry,

then checked his height again.

It was still the same.

"You're just as special as your cousin," said his mother,
but Junior didn't believe her. Kong was on Broadway . . .

he was in a movie . . .

*and* he was grand marshal of
the Thanksgiving Day Parade.

Junior and Bernice watched him pass by.

Well, Junior did.
Bernice was suddenly nowhere to be found.

Then Junior heard a terrible howling.
Bernice was stuck in a tree!

Without thinking, Junior climbed
up to get her, but when he looked
down, the ground was very far away.

Still, it was Thanksgiving, and Junior was hungry,
so he draped Bernice over his shoulders and scooched
down to the ground.

Dinner was wonderful.

"You were very brave today," said
Junior's mother at bedtime.

Junior did not feel brave, exactly,
but he did feel warm and happy.

And maybe even . . .